# The Honey

*by Zeina B. Ghandour*

Interlink Books

An imprint of Interlink Publishing Group, Inc.
Northampton, Massachusetts

This edition first published in 2008 by

INTERLINK BOOKS
An imprint of Interlink Publishing Group, Inc.
46 Crosby Street, Northampton, MA 01060
**www.interlinkbooks.com**

Originally published in 1999 by Quartet Books Limited

ISBN: 978-1-56656-719-0

*Cover painting*: Maha Abu-Ayyash
Reproduced by permission of Resistance Art: www.resistanceart.com

Printed and bound in the United States of America

# Contents

# Glossary

abu                    father of

adhan             Islamic call to prayer performed from the minaret of a mosque by the mu'ezzin at dawn, noon, mid-afternoon (as the sun begins its decent), sunset and nightfall. Women may perform the adhan in private in the company of other women alone, and therefore in a subdued voice

ahlan wa sahlan!    Welcome!

ahmar             red (al-Ahmar the red one)

al-Aqsa          the Golden Dome Mosque in the Old City of Jerusalem, where the Prophet Muhammad began his Night Journey to Mecca on a winged horse

ashkar             describes a blond or fair-skinned man (al-Ashkar the blond or fair one)

| | |
|---|---|
| *asrar* | secrets |
| *awra* | taboo |
| *Eid* | festival, religious holiday or celebration |
| *farhan* | happy, joyful |
| *hijab* | veil worn by Muslim women to cover their hair and preserve their modesty. For Sufis, a *mouhajjab* is a person who is governed by intellect or emotion and who is therefore unable to access immaterial consciousness. Amulets inscribed in holy verses to shield one from curses are also called *hijab* |
| *hurra* | free woman |
| *jinn* | According to Islamic belief, *jinn* are malevolent spirits who live in underground channels and who have the capacity to wreak havoc in the lives of human beings |

| | |
|---|---|
| Judaea and Samaria | Old Testament term for the west bank of the Jordan River (the West Bank), which forms part of Palestine and which has been illegally occupied by Israel since 1967. Arab residents of the West Bank need Israeli permits to enter Occupied East Jerusalem and Inside, or Israel proper |
| *kafiya* | traditional thick checked cotton scarf worn by Palestinian men. The colour of the kafiya (red or black) was used during the Palestinian Uprising to denote political allegiance. |
| *kippa* (also *yarmulke*) | Worn by observant Jewish men to cover their head as a sign of respect for God, the Most High |
| *La Ilaaha Illa Allah* | There is only one God |
| *majnouna* | mad or possessed woman |

| | |
|---|---|
| *Maya* | According to Hindu/Buddist tradition, Maya signifies the Veils of Illusion and symbolizes the illusory power of the universe. |
| *mighli* | boiled dessert made of rice flour |
| *mu'ezzin* | a righteous man who calls the faithful to prayer from the Mosque |
| al-Quds | Arabic for Jerusalem – meaning the sanctified city. |
| *radwan* | benevolent, kind or compassionate |
| *ruhiya* | spiritual or soulful woman |
| Salat al-Asr | sunset prayer |
| Salat al-Fajr | dawn prayer |

| | |
|---|---|
| *shaheed* | martyr to Islam; self sacrifice for God. He who bears witness to the Oneness of God is also called *shaheed*. |
| *Shtakhim* | Hebrew term which designates the Palestinian residents of the West Bank, who are living under Israeli military occupation |
| Surat al-Nahl | Verse of the Bees |
| Surat al-Qamar | Verse of the Moon |
| *umm* | mother of |
| *yehya* | life; the will to live |

dedicated

to my blood .

*I want to speak with a non-poetic voice*

*I want to tell it how it is*

Prelude

There was once a mosque that was yellow, and that had to be painted blue. The men in the village where the mosque stood rose at daybreak one day and went about their task with purpose. They had agreed it should be a light blue, the colour of a benevolent sky on a spring day. But they were novices. They neglected to apply a coat of white paint and only after the paint had dried did they realize the mosque had come out green. They laid their brushes aside for a few days and put away the paint, tried to love the new colour. Eventually though, they had to concede that the green was reminiscent of the yellow they had tried to cover, and of the blue they failed to achieve. There was no need for any conferring, for their unease drew them again to the mosque, where they rolled up their sleeves one evening and smiled knowing smiles. This time, the men underestimated the darkness, and it eclipsed their vision, and the next morning the navy walls of the mosque stood like a dark stain against the summer day in the village of al-Ahmar.

They went on like this for many days, stripping their fresh coats of colour, mixing, repainting. The mosque was painted electric blue, midnight and indigo. When they finally achieved the desired colour, they were so absorbed by their task that they failed to recognize it, and painted it lilac. The women in the village did not speak, feigning not to notice the vacant ritual. Finally the men became despondent, declared that the mosque was beyond restoration, should be painted red, like the earth on which it stood, and left alone. They dispersed with glum expressions and heavy arms to their homes and to a quiet communal prayer, even though it was not a Friday. The general feeling that there had been a failure to atone and make amends hung on through the night to the next morning, when the first family left al-Ahmar.

With time, the entire village was deserted, for the men were unable to bear the permanent reminder that they had blundered on a hallowed place.

The mosque stands there still, though it is not forsaken. On moonless nights a strange creature, half-bird half-woman, appears at the top of the minaret to sing her song. They call her the desert mermaid, and she performs the call to the dawn prayer. Those who have heard her say that her voice is so luminous, it was as though the sun and moon both had been arrested in it. And those who have seen her say they have been dazzled. They describe yellow hair and brown skin, and eyes that seem to have been wired by a mesh of lightning.

It is said that nothing requested of the trapped soul is too much trouble, that she is the source of the spring which feeds the oasis and that her smile would resonate in your heart long after tears of joy had streamed down to your feet upon hearing her voice, as you stood at the bottom of the minaret.

Yet the mere mention of her name, Ruhiya, evokes a fear dark and rare like black coral, and deep and mysterious as the sea which contains it.

It is a firm heart which comes to her in need. For it has been verified that should the whim strike her, Ruhiya will distil your spirit from your flesh.

# Ruhiya's Song

*Bid'a*

*deviant act; the irreverent breach of
a sacred tradition*

## Ruhiya

*Spirit or flesh. How do I honour my love? When I look upon his face I see it timelessly as God. I could eat fire with him, trample on hot coals, store water like a camel and run towards death prepared. I closed my eyes into his heart long ago and watched it darken from the inside, where he held me, cradled like a last glimmer of hope.*

Radwan's brow was soaked with sweat, his cheeks were wet with tears.

'I haven't missed one *adhan* in thirty years...'

'Shush...my son.' Umm Radwan laid her plump, warm hands on her son's frightened face. Shush...' She pulled him up gently and brought a cup of sage tea to his lips, rocking him against her chest as though he had just been born. She looked over at her granddaughter who had fallen asleep with the open Qur'an on her lap. The white cotton *hijab* she usually wore had slipped to the floor, and her feet were tucked in underneath her. Ruhiya was by the window, where she had sat to catch the last rays of the late desert light and read her father's favourite verses out to him as the fever settled into his ailing frame. He had always loved her voice and complimented her on it. He even joked that had she been a boy, she would have taken over from him as the village *muezzin*. Now the sky was moonless and the candles were all spent. The stars shimmered on outside. She lay against the wooden frame of the open window, her right hand resting on the open page at Surat al-Qamar. She had started to read *'the hour is nigh and the moon was cleft asunder'* (Qur'an 54:1) and dozed off hours ago, peacefully between two crescents as the setting moon slid down the sky through the window and was reflected in the mirror on the wall. Sensing her grandmother's gaze on her she opened her eyes, and was immediately reassured by the sound of her father's breathing. She shut the book gently, brought it to her lips for blessing and raised the mother-of-pearl-encrusted cover to her forehead. Radwan had bought it in Bethlehem and given it to Hurra, her mother, on their wedding a few days before the Israeli troops made it their home in the summer of 1967, thirty years ago. The young bride had stood facing her bridegroom on the hill overlooking her birthplace and declared that there was only one God and that Muhammad was his prophet, right there, beneath the tower of the Church of the Nativity. The love-struck, impassioned Radwan had looked into her eyes and seen interminable fields of wild lavender.

'I will boil some more sage,' Ruhiya said to her grandmother, her eyes transfixed by the indentation in the air around the once huge man.

*I am worried about Yehya. He threw away his red kafiya. He said he no longer needed men's doctrines. All he needed was in the Holy Book, including communism. The way he said Holy Book scared me, it made me want to run from him. But he said within it was contained real political opposition and that God was on the side of the radical groups. He threw away the scarf, lest he be mistaken for a communist, or worse, a royalist. Then he exchanged his clothes for trousers with large pockets, that slid to rest on his narrow hips, and honoured the crown of his head with a white crochet cap. He said now his uniform was for real, now he was for real, and stopped shaving. I gave him the veil that he had torn so many times from my head and wrapped it around his neck and told him that I didn't know about men's doctrines but that he should treasure it, and wear it to keep him warm.*

Ruhiya walked back into the room with a pot of fresh tea and a bowl of raw honey brought as a gift from Yehya's father's beehives. The young girl sat between her father and grandmother and began to spoon some honey into his dry mouth.

'Come on, father, just this little bit. We have to get your voice strong so you can sing again, sing again to the whole village.'

His daughter's throat was tight with emotion even as she encouraged the *muezzin*. The breeze that had stirred the palm tops had subsided, leaving the weight of the atmosphere and the smell of hot sand and rocks to drift in from the open window and fill the silence.

'Ruhiya,' the old man spoke. 'I will not sing tomorrow.'

*It was under a lemon tree that Yehya kissed me, in the spring. We were both fourteen. I had been greeting the blossoms when he sneaked up behind me and pulled off my new veil, ironed and embroidered only yesterday by my grandmother. He made me blush. I grabbed it back from him. 'Your hair doesn't look any different from the way it did yesterday.' I stood still and he stood closer.*

'Now you can feel the air on your neck like me,' he said; 'don't you want to be like me?'

I had known before and I knew again that I would live and die with Yehya, that a lifetime on this earth was not enough time together and that maybe eternity, maybe heaven stood a chance of doing justice to our love. But I could never be like him again, since little rivulets of my blood had come between us, as surely as a ravine running through cliff walls.

We had come of age. I heard things about his father, the Honeyman, that I didn't understand, and that he couldn't explain. He kept quiet whenever I asked, What about your father, Yehya? We stopped playing together. He was pulled into the Qur'anic school and started correcting my prayers. He said the verses had to be recited in a certain way because they were eternal and you must pause between words for the exact split second and that was how you knew that you were holding something sacred. Now he's gone again and I can't find him. It's been six weeks since he disappeared with his new clothes, a sprawling beard across his face and his sad, intense friend Eid. I would know if he was dead. Nobody believes he's dead. Twice now I've lost him to God.

Dawn would be breaking soon and there was no sign of the *muezzin* recovering. The small oasis village had heard him call them to prayer without fail five times a day for the last thirty years. He had arrived in the desert with his new wife Hurra, a woman of equal pride and devotion, whose language was filled with superstition, who burnt her Orthodox church's thick incense on every Muslim holy day and who seemed to glide over the ground as she walked.

They thought her barren for many years until the charms and potions prescribed her by the holy man al-Ashkar started to work their magic: in her thirty-third year, ten years after she had married, Hurra finally conceived. And then the baby girl came, in a serene birth so pleasurable for the mother she herself ululated before the umbilical cord was cut. None the less the women who came to her bedside felt they had to console her for failing to produce a successor to the *muezzin*. They brought *mighli*, the traditional sweet usually reserved for the birth of a boy and silver couplets, but they stopped short of congratulating her. Instead they said, 'Thank God for your safety. If you can give birth to a girl, you can give birth to a boy.' Hurra kept quiet. She did not want to tell them that as sure as rebirth followed death she would not have another child, nor that the girl already had a brother. Neither did their condolences dim the brilliance of the love she immediately felt for the baby. Instead she courteously replied to the astounded villagers that she had been hoping for a girl all along, and announced her daughter's name Ruhiya, an ancient pagan name unknown to any of the monotheistic religions, and defied them all to raise the flag of scandal about the *muezzin*'s wife. And they did. They quoted from Surat al-Nahl: '*And they assign daughters for Allah, Glory be to Him!*' (Qur'an 16:57), referring to their pagan ancestors, who called angels the daughters of God.

As the little girl grew up, some noticed the directness of her gaze and commented on her unwillingness to drop it. The more avid gossips said her eyes shone brighter at night and that they darkened into a deep red gold, like those of a fox on the prowl. It was true that Ruhiya was often heard in conversation with inanimate objects, with tables and chairs, with food and flowers, earnestly asking after their feelings. Even though they could not prove that she was emulating her mother with such behaviour, they were sure she was not being scolded for it.

Things changed after her mother's death. Ruhiya missed the amulets inscribed with holy verses and psalms by the holy man al-Ashkar that she used to find hidden by her mother in all corners of the house. The little leather booklets soaked in water, her mother said were written in light. For Hurra had a proverb and a talisman, a folkloric mystical solution for every situation that manifested itself in their house. She spoke of snakes hidden in the shortest grass and of roads invisible in daylight. She used to say, God will show you the path and guide your chosen journey, regardless of how occult it might seem at the beginning.' Even the fluorescent figures who had filed into her room night after night ever since she could remember stopped visiting. The stick people with their neon limbs might have terrified any other child, but Ruhiya understood their language, saw straight into their bottomless eyes and insisted that her bedroom door be kept ajar every night to let them in. The red and green and orange ghosts had come a few times after her mother passed on, to reassure her and calm her sobs. But slowly they grew faint and eventually disappeared.

They were here now. She could make out their skeletal shapes, huddled in the corner, sitting on her mother's bed, and heard them whispering in their breathless tones, transmitting cryptic words into her burning ears.

'Ruhiya, the whole village is going to sleep through the dawn prayer.'

Her father's voice brought her back to him and the figures were spirited away. Umm Radwan was losing hope. The doctor had said the fever had to get worse before it dissipated, but she felt her son weakening; his voice was barely audible. She laid her hand on the Qur'an for comfort and picked it up from the bedside table.

'Ruhiya, listen to me; go and wake al-Ashkar, tell him I am unwell, and that he should call the *adhan* for me. It's no time for tears, my daughter, I am only getting closer to God. Hush now, don't cry, it's nearly daybreak; hurry, Ruhiya, I will be here when you get back.'

*My grandmother kept a large bottle of lavender water, an embroidered handkerchief and a hairbrush on her white dresser. My heart sank every time she began her ablutions because I was about to lose her to her meditation, when God would have her absolute attention, and I would be required to* sit quietly on the bed and I would hold my breath so as not to disturb her. I tried to tell her that her prayers were interminable and that God must know her by now; she didn't need to remind him that she loved him so many times a day, did she? She would smile and cover me with kisses and say, 'If you forget God, God will forget you.' Still, I was impatient for the final greeting, 'May God's peace and mercy be upon you,' whispered to the angels on her shoulders. How I loved that last ritual, after which my poise and composure would be rewarded by stories as she fed me almonds and figs, and we renewed the intimacy that had been interrupted by her remembrance.

And what if God had already forgotten me? I was too young to pray and worried that by the time I was old enough, God may have forgotten that he had ever created me. 'Ruhiya knows God, and God knows Ruhiya' became my private prayer; 'Ruhiya knows God, and God knows Ruhiya.' I said it in my prayers, I said it in my sleep, I said it and said it. Then I started to call the adhan every time I prayed, because I read that this was permissible, as long as it was performed in private. I liked the way my voice sounded and unconsciously began to raise it.

*I raised it and raised it, aiming for the sky. And like our prophet, who once prayed to Jerusalem, I turned west to al-Quds, instead of south, to Mecca. I closed my eyes and looked for al-Aqsa, the Further Mosque, the Golden Dome that shines like God's heart in the centre of the Old City. Even Yehya didn't know whether to praise or curse me, but in the end he said, 'Jerusalem needs all the prayers it can get but you're taking your chances with God.' I stopped – though I'm facing al-Quds now because I know this is where he is gone, and where he wants to die.*

Ruhiya stepped out of the stone house clutching her veil, the gentle breeze against her. She began to tie her hair back but then changed her mind. The night would conceal her, sleep would stand guard. Defiantly she wrapped the *hijab* around her waist. It had been years since she felt the wind at the nape of her neck, coolness dispersing the midsummer sweat beads. She dragged her bare feet along warm sand. The house of al-Ashkar was on the other side of the village. The breeze had picked up and swayed the tall palms to its murmur. As her mother promised, another path appeared before her. She turned around and headed for the mosque, guided by the flamboyant bougainvillaea trees and the rows of jasmine. She looked up at the sky and at the bright dots in it. They formed a swirling crown for the yellow mosque. They peeked through the waxing and waning moon carved in its stone wall. The door was wide open as always and the steps to the minaret were just beyond it. The stairway seemed too narrow for her father's square frame, too dark. His sunken face was in front of her. His eyes blinked once and then disappeared. Her feet led her up the steps. The smell of his musk was all around. Could her father's song be more melancholic? It had been agreed from the first day that the yearning in the young Radwan's voice was unmatched. And it had grown more poignant still as the years went by. Noticing, the villagers said: 'Listen to the *muezzin*, longing some more.' And as the years went by, they too were swept along in the longing and in the twilight hours of the day, at sunrise, at sunset, his call to prayer flooded their eyes with phantom tears.

She stood at the top of the minaret, alone on the circular balcony. The breeze was even cooler up here and the whispering had stopped. She looked around her and saw the rooftops of the houses of al-Ahmar for the first time. The branches on the trees formed ghostly shadows against the sky. The song in her throat had swollen like an abscess and drenched her in sweat. She pulled her veil up to her shoulders and wiped her face with it. She thought of Umm Kulthum, the Egyptian diva with the power to silence a nation with her song. Why was that woman's voice not *awra*? Ruhiya's grandmother told her that even in Jerusalem Umm Kulthum quietened entire neighbourhoods when she was on the radio, from Ras al-Amud to the Orthodox Quarter in the Old City, and that old men would sit twirling their moustaches and twisting their water-pipes pensively at her ballads. She told Ruhiya that from the money-changers and barber-shops on Salaheddin Street to the university campuses in Bethlehem and Birzeit, eyes closed in dreamy contemplation at her songs. And that there was never any trouble from the soldiers when Umm Kulthum sang. Because her songs were from the heart.

It was moments to the dawn prayer. The sky defrosted coolly as the sun waited below the horizon. She closed her eyes and crossed the desert to a sparkling sea. There was a time when speaking was forbidden, and it seemed so long ago.

*I am bloated right now with the love God has shown me. But nothing has changed; I just am where I should be, holding my breath for an intrepid amount of time and asking the morning if she will be mine. Stand by me as I praise His greatness.'*

'*Allaahu Akbar!*' Her body was stiff. The yell had escaped from her. She stood steadfast as a volcano disgorging boiling liquid, dispensing words like ashes. Ruhiya savoured them like sweets dissolving beneath her tongue. At the end, with Yehya in mind, she paused correctly: '*La Ilaaha Illa Allah...*' There is no other God but me.

Ruhiya opened her eyes and put her hand on her heart. She looked down. A little girl was standing below by the minaret and looking up at her. It was Asrar, the daughter of the holy man and healer al-Ashkar. Ruhiya had not seen her until that moment but now their eyes interlocked with mutual love and gratitude. Ruhiya pressed her hand to her lips as if inspecting a fresh wound. Her mouth bore no traces of shame, despite the slight tremor and the tingling beneath her skin. Mindfully she turned away and went inside, then ran down the steps of the minaret and back out of the mosque. She walked up to the little girl standing outside and knelt down so they were face to face. The two, one on the verge of womanhood and the other who had just released herself from its constraints so sensationally, stared at each other like two cats from a different breed. Ruhiya spoke first.

'Asrar, you must not repeat what you saw. You must keep it to yourself. Cross your heart and swear on the Qur'an that you will keep it to yourself.'

'I would swear on the Qur'an, the Cross, the Torah. I would swear but everybody has already heard you, Ruhiya.'

Ruhiya smiled. She spoke softly: 'Including God?'

Asrar looked at the young woman kneeling in front of her without answering. She knew she had just witnessed something significant, but she did not fully understand the reason behind the panic in Ruhiya's eyes.

'God forgive me! You have to keep my secret, Asrar.'

Asrar did not hesitate. 'You are the secret,

Ruhiya.' For if there was one thing Asrar recognized, it was secrets.

This was a first in the village of al-Ahmar. Never before had the call to the dawn prayer been howled and moaned with this much pleasure. And in their sleep, the villagers were willing to overlook the fact that it was being sung by a woman. But when they were woken that morning by Ruhiya's song, they stumbled out of their beds and ran out into their gardens with dread and disbelief. For the women immediately knew she would pay for this pleasure, even though it had been so gracefully displayed. And the men? The men felt her song pierce through their hearts like a burning spear.

Yet there was nothing vulgar or brazen about her. She was like some exotic bird that had come down to rest from her flight. And the hardest thing to get used to was that nothing could have prepared them for the gratification and delight they felt on hearing her, or for the sweetness that lingered on in the atmosphere of her song at mid-morning.

## NIGHTFALL
# Yehya's Journey

*Nushuz*

*that which tries to elevate itself*
*above ground*

## Yehya

The explosives they gave me are weightless. Kilograms of unquantifiable material, butterflies in bushes to my heart. I can run around with them on my back, on my hips, in a bag, I could wear them in my shoes, strap them under my arms, balance them on my head. They're cotton wool, they're candy floss, they're for children, they're lightweight with wings. On which I ride I fly I die.

They add nothing to my gait. Nothing to my stride, still long and light into the pitch-black recesses of their sleep. I reach them through the night. They don't know me now, can't see me. I am them, transformed. I am the clamour and the tuneless song. A free animal, I have a destiny and a vision. My life acquires its meaning when I die. I am dying with every emotion. I'm finished. I am my breath. And my breath is about to explode.

Jerusalem looks like a rotten peach. An imprint of fire on my belly like the criminal record I cannot spend. A crooked twisted broken limb, crippled by them like my right hand, hanging there on the edge of my wrist so useless, so useless, that I have to pick up the Holy Book with my left hand, turn its fragrant pages with my left hand. I carry the

33

screaming and the memories and I prepare to lay them down. I carry my mother's face with me the night they dragged me away, a crying boy, and brought me back a beast of blood. I carry it with me so I can lay it down. The one who laughed as I cried, who moved like an elevator and hummed like one, I carry him with me and will lay him down. I am the sum total. I want them to see the parts.

The languid border police on the corner can't see me at all. They mistake me for a New Native, delighted by their bravery, their colours, their geography, their nonchalance as they recline against the old uneven walls, knees ajar, dream metal between their legs. What care do I take when I walk past you? I fragment my walk, disjoin my grace, before anyone picks up on the anger in my hip swing. I smile to myself. I am a bundle of contraband anger, smuggled in, here to stay in a form you dread, to be embedded in your genetic memory for ever and ever, on to your innocents now, this is the enchanted night-time walk.

In a few hours I will meet Eid and we will not say a word to each other...but if I see him slouching with the importance of what he carries, the consequence on his shoulders? Will I look up at the sky and breathe it to him, straighten my shoulders and stretch my spine up for him? Like Quetzalcoatl, the Mayan eagle-snake, we will conquer our base nature and fly with the higher spirit. Will I even recognize him by the Old City ramparts in his black clothes and high hat? He said he would be looking up at the Mount of Olives, where he was born, and that he would be weeping. We will arrange ourselves like two cockerels because the money is on us. And finally to reach the point of love, the summit of healing, the centre of softness. A thin oily film is sealing every pore, every orifice, every wound so that I slip through the night on a path illuminated by a crescent moon, a disinterested cockroach, my belly to the earth, my back to the sky.

I have never known such calm. There is only garbage and fat cats, quiet and quick. There is the rustling of nuns' robes and Eastern European whisperings. Gusts of fresh night air push me around that corner and then down this street, through city gates and invisible borders and I am light, light like laughter trapped in a cave.

The walls are observed, the borders have ears. Every step I take is a checkpoint to be transcended.

Every beat of my heart is a danger sign. Still alive, still weak, still striving. My veins are a sophisticated network of surveillance spies mapping out my journey. No matter where you take refuge you will hear me. I will resound acoustically. Your whole being will receive me, I will come through cool and crisp.

Who is stomping on my territory unprepared?

Was there a time when I didn't know her? Was there a time when I knew her better? I've been deaf to Ruhiya's pleading but I can hear her now, chirping my name like a little bird that has swallowed grass, squeaking through the cracks of light in the sky. She who ran uncharted, through visionary mazes in the desert to another oasis, ran barefoot on burning sand, reminded me to keep the safety latch on any weapon I came across. Ritualistically, I turned to my brethren. But she couldn't see my tears for the width of my shoulders. I turned my back to her with revulsion, a convulsive, sobbing sky inside me. She cried after me: 'You are the Keeper of the Tombs, Yehya! You don't deserve your beautiful name,' and I knew she was making it easier for me to leave.

The hanging smell of amber is all over, all around me. Eid must be nearby. Eid's hand-dipped incense and smoky sandalwood oil had given his mother and father hope, that the scents of his craft would lull and overcome him with their kindness. Eid made orange and camomile soap that was said to heal old scars and clear dark memories. But even as golden saffron stained his hands and cinnamon warmed his winters, Eid dried up inside.

Where is he?

I can smell his sweet blood now, almost hear his breathing as he muscles up to his destiny. He's fragrant, he can't help it, a flower in bloom, his heart open and itchy for all to scratch. I must cluster to him. Two mutating cells in a dilapidated body.

And all the while the silence, the strange silence of Jerusalem at night.

Sometimes she used to sing. She would raise her voice in prayer ever so slightly so as not to be heard in the next room and then reprimand herself, sternly and loudly: 'My voice is taboo.' Harshly she would repeat her admonishment, disbelieving it from her core. 'Does my voice stir you, Yehya? Am I prompting you to sin?' Yes, yes, Ruhiya, your voice creates a disorder and an agitation inside me and I wish I could fly with the same grace and not choke with this despair. We used to play a game, where she resolved that she was a seagull and I was the sea and she could sing as long and loud as she pleased and I lapped the shores and drowned in bottomless expanse, indifferently. A falling moon, a moving star, a nightlight on the beach. She was in and on me, until I was Ruhiya and Ruhiya was me. But soon she was forever interrupting my anxiety, like a distracting sprinkling of sugar on my nightmares, repeating that I didn't need proof, didn't need more proof about God, didn't need to materialize my love for him or corroborate his words with sound-bites and dogma. I had stopped feeling pain, I had stopped expecting terrors. The injustice fell away like a badly formed idea and the shouting in my ear stopped and the burns miraculously healed. My body stopped remembering, reminding. Finally I could access peace and Ruhiya distracted me. She gave me a silver signet ring for my transformation and threw one of her veils over my shoulders. She said she would no longer interrupt my meditation and let it take me where it will and her eyes swelled suddenly with tears of certain knowledge that her love meant nothing and that I was leaving 'You are entitled to subterfuge, you are entitled to the occult. You are not entitled to anger or joy or pleasure. This is your decision, Yehya, and this is how you have lived and this is how you will die. You are like me. You're wearing a veil but it's your heart that's hid in it and you will not be discovered until it is too late. You're an intellectual, Yehya.'

I see Eid. I never knew it was possible for my blood to tremble so, to sizzle like embers inside me, an ageing and spent volcano. In the twilight of my last hour, of the last calm before another mayhem, of the listless, dark dawn before it's time for prayer, my dread is real and my heart is famished. One of us will betray the other, as it is always in hell on earth. Damascus Gate is behind me, Paradise in front. Still in the Arab side of the city where the taxis begin to gather, basketfuls of ripe fruit to unload, familiar faces to unfold for a distant sun. Heading west and our victims are upon me, my intimates, my playmates, my blood brothers in the last moment of the sweet interlude of life. All converges here on the old Greenline, a continually seeping wound continually stitched and bled. The forbidden intersection for me, the open door for them. Where I speak their language and they swear in mine. Where I ooze on to them from an infected laceration. Where I stop nibbling senseless, like a maggot on a corpse.

Where I explode and maim the one who stands beside me.

On Fridays the faithful curse all the way to al-Aqsa, unstoppably pouring in from the severed countryside as stubbornly as arteries reconnecting with a healthy heart. From beyond the threshold of the zoo, they knock down portals and doorways, they bend bars and squeeze out like gorillas evolving around a sudden consciousness. They forge trails of backroads and backalleys, instinctively as primates teetering on familiar terrain.

My seagull is upon me, circling the sky. What is she doing here, a good few checkpoints to the next beach? Bidding me to join her and slip out to sea. The car awaits me. A plastic skull hangs from the rear-view mirror. The bald boy in heavy golden chains didn't look at me as I dived in but his elbow jerked slightly and he wiped the palm of his hand on the red velvet seat.

'Do you believe in fate?' he asked me as we pulled up to a traffic light.

'My name is Yehya,' I say to him, since I can't imagine another answer.

'I'm Shaheed.' He turned to me finally, although his eyes couldn't sustain my stare.

Friday morning how I greet you. Loaded like a mule. With bound wrists and ankles. As I step out of the car with my head up, acerbic curses are loud within me. I stumble along as I did on parched desert rocks, recall the nectar that I drank from her cupped hand. Is that a Jew I see before me? He doesn't look like one. He doesn't look like the Jews I know. A black-eyed boy, still as a hawk. I've crossed my tribe and several others, men from my region and his father's brothers, to find where he was at. To meet him here on this playground skullcap to skullcap and turn iron into mud. To die together a death with social significance and create a political moment.

A sand-encrusted wind laps my brittle back.

My seagull is upon me again, screaming her allegiance to a sky so faithful, I can hear the echo of her spirit's laughter. Ruhiya, my father's daughter, my sister reclaiming me with her song.

The moon is long gone, martyrdom and murder are close. A frosty light has absorbed the shadows I occupied. Yehya, the shepherd of death, the reluctant sacrifice. My pulse is betraying me, my brother is in front. Soon we will reach the Neutral Terrain, where we create Difficulty. Soon we become entangled, once and forever, with enemy flesh. Soon we manifest the hateful alliance scientifically, biologically. Our hearts and our passions will be forcibly exhibited. Our poison, our intoxication, soberly received by pirates and thieves.

Then they will know that the cannibals had started feasting, well before the feast.

But my seagull is upon me, drowning me in song, ripping my insides with her beak till I drop my weights and fly. We'd been patient within the walls, we've thrived in badlands like weeds. It's time for the final homage. I hear Eid's blessing to the wind that blew him like a fire on a rampage to the bleak landscape. I hear the gratitude and dread and choke on my own defeat. A faraway explosion ripped the ground beneath my feet and I could smell his incinerated heart from all the others.

Palestine! Babylon is in flames.

Who will stand witness to this agony, this journey? My seagull is on me, leading the retracted pilgrimage, the treacherous way home I traced as a martyr and retrace as a refugee.

Now I'm in a bit of a fix. I sense the doors open, I sense the doors close. Jerusalem is but a stone city with a heart of gold. Home of the sacred and the profane. Where my will was consecrated, where my action is defiled.

The sky is pouring its honey along the Old City walls and I am again one of its subterranean rodents, still alive, still weak, still striving. It's time after all for *Salat al-Fajr* and I turn south and kneel down, wondering how many ablutions it will take to rinse my unclean heart.

The divided, impossible city that sang to me at dawn, we are under siege.

# Retreat

*Ta'arrud*

*to barricade; also refers to men initiating sexual disorder, by placing themselves in front of women and making improper suggestions*

## Maya

A day of bombing is not unlike a festival day: road blocks and barricades at every step, sudden demonstrations, mounted riot police and gigantic Closures, and checkpoints circling the suburbs like Christmas lights. Despite all of which, I sense the definite and barely repressed spring in the step of the Arab residents of the Old City, Jerusalem, and the trilling, celebratory eyes all round. I don't mean to shock and I shock even myself but for the Israelis the ones that they call *Shtakhim*, the West Bankers of their nightmares, are undead again. It's the return of the prodigal son from the land of the settlers, it's the unsilenceable meek inheriting, the claim to Judaea and Samaria and even the coastline. Every potential terrorist finally is and can take pride. I have a foreign passport to go with my wild blond hair, to carry with my mace spray and matt lipstick in the same handbag. I'm an emissary of foreign reason, dispassionate intellect and ethical reportage. It's business as usual for me until either the career break, or the manic episode.

Until then, I've got myself into a clinch with this city; I'm on the air, all boys, and I'm rolling with the energy.

*A streetboy to end all streetboys. A boy rough like caustic soda. Tender like cotton, strained like a drum. I really wanted to see him snap. It quickly became obvious that his Hebrew was impeccable and that he was on first name terms with the big boys and other enforcers around the Old City. He walked towards me with a hunch in his shoulder that late summer day as I leant against the new railings at Jaffa Gate. He smiled a wretched smile and stood invadingly, envelopingly close.*

*I was recently returned from Africa, I was still on a slow burn. A brown suede dress kept me cool in the midday sun. I tingled with the residue of salt on my skin and dreamt of floating, meditating, under the water. He looked at me as if to say, 'I think we both want to,' and all the caution of the last three years disappeared in my smile. It was time to let my hair down and I wanted to let it down all over that man's stomach. Still, I allowed him to cajole me, and to write down my phone number between two insults. He called late the same night on the road from somewhere and pressed me into a midnight date, pinned me up against a wall later and threatened me, silently, into his stone-cold room and narrow stone bed.*

Oh People! This bombing is special: so close to the Arab side of the city, the rotten East Side, just west of one monument, down the road from another. So close, someone is getting desperate. And in addition, there is titillating talk of a botched second suicide. An escapee of his own fate, a magician, a sorcerer for good measure. So we're stuck with a hat trick for this month, September gets three. I know what to look for, what the readers will lap up: the random limbs and the innocents (babies, Arabs, Romanian labourers, all suddenly innocent). My lord and the chaos of singed skin and indistinguishable parts. The Orthodox Jews recuperating muscle and bone and organs blown to high heaven, into the trees. And in between the lines I will utter: Surely this isn't Zion. Climbing trees with rubber gloves and plastic bags in hand to reassemble the dead. These are my notes and I could have copied them straight from the last time. 1997, nightmare in Zion.

Where I could perish. Where I wish I would perish though I'm alive and kicking praises to God so I can't indulge. Maybe it's not really an option, because I am not an innocent. I am an edge-hugging risk-taker of exaggerated risks. The unwritten article is rubber-stamped, anyhow, courtesy of

Donor Countries and Peace Brokers. I recall a reggae song *Aid Travels with a Bomb*.

Jesus wept last week in the Church of the Nativity in Bethlehem, and the witness to the miracle swore it was drops of blood that fell from His eyes. I went to see for myself and stood with Greek tourists and camcorders but I never saw Him cry. I didn't see him blink. I later asked God for forgiveness for surreptitiously having sought a sign of His existence.

*I should have put a stop to this when I still could. The late-night calls reverberated and the man's drawl at 1 a.m. terrified me. Of course he lied. He lied, I'm quite sure, about everything. He was known by one syllable, Heed. But he wrote his name down in full for me. Here, this is my middle name. Tribalistically – as if to say, that's who I am, this is my father and this here is his granddaddy and I have nothing to hide. To me he was Heed, the baldhead. Stay on his good side.*

*This is my father. This is my tribe.*

I stopped by the Arab bus station, at a grocery store that stocks everything. I want to make linguine and broccoli with sun-dried tomatoes. I want to throw in cheese that is Italian if I can find some and I'm in the right place to look. I want to peel and grate a root vegetable, but is it the season for roots? The store is owned by an Armenian family and one of their sons was tending the till, a small gold cross glistening on his chest. I walk up to him with Dinner on my mind.

Something was making me queasy and I don't know if it's the adrenalin or the disgust. This morning there was enough carnage on my doorstep to render the daylight obscene. Yet somehow on Jaffa Road I managed to stop to order a cream-cheese bagel with sesame and onion for breakfast on my way back, and ate on the go. I bit off and chewed the soft sweet dough absentmindedly like a grazing little lamb. The third bomb on the fifteenth breakfast of the ninth month. I strolled towards Damascus Gate as if I was in Turin. Of the dozens of louche boys effortlessly loitering today nobody grabs me although I'm surprised by an unusually lyrical reference to my creaminess. Oh the boys, oh God. So slithery I'm repeatedly surprised that handcuffs don't slide right off their wrists. So slippery, just slide down them! I hear beautiful words. Somebody says Pomegranate. The poesy of the Bedouins lies latent in their prose, but their eyes promise the deepest disrespect and threaten to deliver it. Though I wear an armour with no detectable openings, the boys don't need any come-on besides a sign of life. But I know and love the danger of Israel and I exorcise it in bold: **Bombing in Jerusalem, How many Dead?** Grinding along nicely if all goes well and next week will be: **Bombing Prompts Brutal Closure**. And then the wind-down, **Suicide Bomber Identified**. Names and numbers will change, and I will slot them in like a factory worker. My Arab friends will say no justice no peace and my Jewish friends will say these were civilians. Then the sitters around tables will take over the floor and attempt to harness the shockwaves sent through their system. And I will quote them all in italics.

In the meantime I sleep with a twenty-two-year-old Arab Jerusalemite, a certain collaborator who makes love to me in Hebrew in a voice that daunts me until I say baby, please, baby me in the mother tongue.

*'Maya, call the office. We think we know the first name of the bomber, it's Eid, and he's from a place*

*called al-Ahmar, near Jericho. The West Bank and*
*Gaza are sealed but for the moment Palestinians*
*are still being allowed to return to their*
*hometowns. We're arranging for a car to drive you*
*down to al-Ahmar this morning. Call. Oh*
*and... There's a funny rumour going round of some*
*crazy woman who called the* adhan *this dawn at the*
*same village, at the same time as the bomb went*
*off.'*

The sea is to the west, the desert to the east. I stand
right here on the frontline, the Greenline; I live
beyond the wall, within the stones by Damascus
Gate, and I get to the New Gate by walking along
the Via Dolorosa, where Jesus walked, where
pilgrims walk the path of devotion. Past the Eighth
Station of the Cross where he stopped, and spoke to
the daughters of Jerusalem. Cry for yourselves not
me, he said. And fell again. And I write about
masked men and terrorists, about diplomats and
deals and detonations. I rehearse my questions in
Arabic and write them down phonetically. This is
one story, not two. This is one story. Though I didn't
know why and for once I was not sure that I would
find out. Nowhere, never, has there been a woman

*muezzin*, a *muezzina*. But there's a Eid every now and then, predictable as my headlines and the festivals of his namesake.

I hadn't anticipated this.

This could lead to an honour killing. Definitely an incarceration of one kind or another, or an expulsion. If they had the means, they would be planning her lobotomy. She will be called *majnouna*, possessed by the *jinn*, the underground spirits of sewers and drains. Then there will have to be an exorcism. It will be way too hot for jeans in the desert so I changed into white linens and a long-sleeved T-shirt. Who will I speak to? The place will be crawling with police and army. There will be starched blue uniforms liaising with battered green uniforms, and scratchy talk on radios. OK. This is Israel, let the games begin. You call our bluff and we will deconstruct you like a metaphor and toy with you like an idea. At this point Palestinians will look like kids at an adults' party. They will act surprised after the fact at the dramatic reaction and whine submissively. Hush the proud men forced to submit to the sound of handcuffs clanking open and shut. I will hear bad Arabic and broken Hebrew and communicate in both, the retrograde Semitic tongues that fly like two falcons against one horizon: it can never be, one will inevitably destroy the other.

I grabbed my swimsuit for a dip in a river on the way back and put it down again. I want to fly back and write. Damn it all.

*He had gentle, dreamy eyes, damn it, that made him look perpetually drunk. But he really couldn't focus on my words and convoluted sentences. He said, 'You should have been an Arab because your mind works strange. It's like the twisted streets and dead-end lanes of this city. 'But sometimes when I let him (let him in, let him through), he came upon an unexpected surprise, a courtyard behind an iron door that held the key to Everything...*

*It's true that since I've been here, I've been losing my symmetry, my nerve. That I have started to drift mid-sentence and to struggle in speech. It was as though my vocabulary had leaked out irrecoverably in osmosis. I was forgetting to speak and how to speak. I had assumed that the alliance between my mouth and brain was irreversible. But I no longer wanted to impart ideas, I wanted to vomit. My words had sunk down to the bottom of my gut, and they were making me sick. I will go soon, once I've uttered the last, so that I can leave completely mute after I'm all out and I can't begin to imagine the laborious recuperation of sounds and grammar again.*

It's Friday morning in the Old City and I can't walk. Instead I get shuffled along its narrow streets by a great surge of bodies behind and in front of me, in tiny baby steps with my arms stuck to my side. I have considered moving to a more genteel neighbourhood, maybe a leafy avenue on the Jewish West Side. But somehow the call to prayer in stereo five times a day held me in its thrall. I stayed. I let the bells of the Holy Sepulchre and the Sunday morning pianos drift through my skylight windows and fill my concrete, haunted spaces. I wondered whether on leaving the Old City, I would have come back simply to sit at Jaffa Gate after the Shabat siren has wailed and wooed the Jews into an inoffensive weekly quietude, and watch Conservative worshippers in all kinds of hats? I used to sit mesmerized on a stone bench by the Tower of David, as they streamed into the Jewish Quarter in the milky sun that I have never seen anywhere else, carrying a prayer book in one hand and an offensive weapon in the other. My camera preyed and captured what it could until one Friday a young man took a long stride towards me until I backed up and shouted in my face: 'Photographing natives?' Nationalism hounding me. I answered, 'The natives of New York maybe,' and the man really looked as if he was going to either cry or hit me, as though I had sadistically planned to confound him.

I waited at the top of the steps of Damascus Gate for the car to pick me up. I act confident and look glamorous. We drove away from the city towards the suburbs of East Jerusalem and headed down into the Jordan Valley, past illegal Israeli settlements, olive groves and Bedouin encampments. Down into the orange and ochre sands of a desert spotted with shrubs of pistachio-green sage, and the occasional spring or stream. The land turned into a deep-red limestone as we approached Wadi al-Nar, Fire Valley. And there, amidst unusual and lush vegetation, stood the village of al-Ahmar.

An unhinged anxiety gnawed at my stomach. It's red. A dark-red red. I felt a sudden urge to peel off my sandals and get this pink sand between my toes. Cinnamon-coloured clouds of dust rose and fell around my feet as I followed the scent to the martyr's house. There, mirrored sunglasses and moustaches were skimming the ground like insects over a swamp in a routine hunt for the usual suspects. Members of the suspected bomber's family had been hauled away, and by the look in the eyes of their neighbours, they too were in for the long haul. Very soon the reprisal would follow and in the rubble of the next house-demolition, revenge would root again. I pulled out my notebook.

The uniforms were acting as if they were tying up loose ends, but this is a point on a circle and they know it. In a matter of hours, the secret police on both sides can start collecting the lard from the Peace Agreements, better understood as Security Arrangements, since these form the essential part of the deal between the Palestine Liberation Organization, now the government, and the Israelis. The only part that both sides are so vigorously dedicated to enforcing. For water and other resources, airports and elections and other similar trappings of statehood, are part of the secondary legislation and form a blurry background on the security map. The focus of the scene is on the primary concern, the military players of the peace brigade. It's about information, communication and codes. Preservation and pragmatism.

Readers, I don't feel like being objective, I'm feeling unrestrained.

So peace-loving Arabs today Talk to the Israelis about self-preservation, and excuse me for getting technical but I in turn have to Talk about that. And this is why, even though the term itself is so combustible, it is these Peace Agreements which will ensure that more young men are bundled up into loose batches of violations and grievances only to be sooner or later, unaccountably, unleashed on to us.

Whilst standing in the crowd I overheard that the door to the yellow mosque was locked and that the *muezzin* had been unable to call the noon prayer. Apart from this my questions were ignored even as probing eyes probed me. Men will steal your energy if you're lucky, devour you if you're not. I put away my pen, I stop asking my questions. Since I have been here, I have learnt to shut off the whispered menaces, the hissing delivered by clammy tongues. I have learnt to side-step suggestive posturing and stay to one side.

The heat was choking me. The stares were suddenly too much for me to bear. Their eyes were dropping on me like drowsy flies and I felt like a swamp lake, a breeding ground for parasites. I shivered despite the heat and left.

As I headed out towards the palace ruins on the edge of the village, I came upon a group of women lounging under the shade of a cypress tree in a front yard. They indicated that they wanted me to come and join them. They sat on woven blankets, surrounded by stacks of cooked vine leaves, bunches of parsley and bowls of rice, meat, tomatoes and nuts.

'Come! Madame! Come. Take photograph!'

'Welcome! Come and sit down. Where from? Norvège?' The ladies were already making room for me on the floor next to them.

'*Ahlan! Ahlan wa sahlan!* What brings you to al-Ahmar? Sit.'

I sat. A little girl opposite me was stroking the kitten on her lap. As she stood up to pour me a glass of lemonade the little animal climbed on to her shoulders. She giggled as she broke off a sprig of fresh mint and dropped it in my glass. Someone was asking me if I was married. I couldn't lie any more, dear God, no, I am not married. That didn't seem to deter the ladies though and as long as there were no men around, the harem felt free to loosen its licentious tongue. Here they use lemons to make lemonade. No detail was spared with regard to the merits and prowess of their men. One young woman was baffled, terrified and repelled by their lively commentary. She was clearly unmarried. I remained quiet so as not to offend my hostesses and feigned disbelief at some of their revelations. In the company of Arab women I felt shy, safe, flirtatious. I developed a sudden sense of modesty and shame. After a while, however, they seemed to tire of the conversation and even appeared to lose interest in me, concentrating again on the vine leaves they had neglected, their afternoon work cut out. I wondered if they were waiting for me to finish my drink and leave.

'Why was there no noon prayer today?'

Silence into words. The oldest one, who had been sitting slightly away from the others surrounded by colourful balls of thick cotton, was working the thread through a skullcap. It looked like a *kippa*. She raised her head to reveal a fleshy, wide face.

'My daughter,' she said in Arabic, 'there was no noon payer and there will be no afternoon prayer in that mosque.'

I caught the eye of the little girl, who was now

standing listening in the doorway, the kitten still confidently perched on her left shoulder. She smiled at me encouragingly.

'But there was a morning prayer in the mosque.'

The old woman's eyes, which had sparkled light-heartedly moments before, now froze in her face and her brow slowly set into a maze of deep furrows. But my curiosity had been stirred.

'I heard that a woman performed the Sheikh's work this morning.' I had spoken tentatively, and lowered my voice.

One of the women looked up. She wiped a sweaty forehead on her sleeve, tossed her head back and laughed heartily. 'Speak up, why are you whispering?' she said. 'Or are you afraid we might hear you?' The others laughed too and I realized I was being gently teased. Seeing me humbled, she gained confidence and continued: 'She performed the Sheikh's work and more . . . ' The woman paused, then looked round to the others to make sure they were still with her on this one. 'What Ruhiya did this morning, it was unbearable. Like pure sugar.'

Then another added: 'Like golden, liquid sugar.'

I looked over at the old lady. Her face had softened somewhat but she was not having any of it. 'Like sugar, like honey. None of you know what you're talking about. Why don't you ask us about 1948? Was your mother born in 1948? We were yanked from our land like bad weeds forty-nine years ago. Smoked like a colony of bees from their hive so they could have the honey in the comb.'

Skilful. Her words were incisive and large and there was no longer any need for subtlety: I was an intruder and a nuisance, to the mourning, to the miracle, to the other, telepathic conversation going on around me. The other women had fallen completely quiet but they remained attentive as they went about the task of rolling tiny perfect little green packages of vine leaves stuffed with the rice mixture. They seemed to take her allusional, collective voice for granted.

'Tell me about this morning. I want to hear it from you.

The old woman laughed. She was gathering the cotton thread around her into separate balls and placing them carefully in a bamboo basket.

'The forty-ninth year is a jubilee for the Jews.

'You don't understand me, do you? That a flower emerges from soil. To appreciate her, you have to taste the mud that sprouts her from its belly. She is

65

the question that had been left to germinate. We are all the result of a violation. And Ruhiya? More than anyone else. That girl has been praying to al-Aqsa all her life, to the Distant Mosque, all Glory be to God... Praying to Jerusalem instead of Mecca, may God forgive me. May He have mercy on my soul for saying it.'

She was talking about the kind of repercussions that I don't write about. I don't write about little waves of consequence that travel like vibrations. The old lady pursed her lips to indicate she had said all she was going to say on the subject. Then, as an afterthought which I suspected was contrived, she added, 'It is Ruhiya you wanted to talk about, isn't it?' When I didn't answer, she picked up the remaining green cotton thread from her lap, and proceeded to add finishing touches to the skullcap. 'But that's how life is,' she said without looking at me, 'sometimes it's bitter, sometimes it's sweet. The forty-ninth year is a jubilee and the fallow land must rest.'

And I knew it was true, that al-Aqsa has become literally, officially unapproachable. The Far Mosque, surrounded by city police, border patrols, the Western Wall and, on Holy Days, by horses and more guns. A resolute patriotism without parallel in the free world. I had come with curiosity, now I felt shame. Come at us with love, or don't come at us at all. I asked for the bathroom just to say something and excused myself.

*How I felt free, and nasty. And what kind of lyrics did he persuade me with? Just, 'Come on, succumb.' And I did, like I was a Dervish and he was my drum. Had I been in love, I would be in love now. The bruises on my skin, the blows to my soul, formed a cyclic calendar. Red, it's Friday, purple Sunday, mauve, blue, Monday, Tuesday. Green, it's Wednesday, Yellow, Thursday. It's Friday again. How I felt with you. I blew up borders for you. I wanted needed had and was finished by you.*

When I went inside I found the little girl crouching in the corner behind the bathroom door with her knees drawn to her chest, the kitten still beside her.

'What's your name, you pretty thing?'

With a slow smile she scooped it into her arms, stood up and raised herself on tiptoes so she could reach my ear. 'Asrar.'

'Is that your real name?'

She didn't answer.

'And what's your cat's name?'

'Cats don't give each other names. They're just cats.' Still standing on the tips of her toes, she had stopped smiling. 'Ruhiya is in the desert, with Yehya,' she said.

'The desert is big, Asrar.'

'You might see them. And if you do, follow them.'

And with that Asrar flew out to the garden, and fluttered into the flowers, like a butterfly.

THE SUN BEGINS ITS DECENT
# Fireflies to the Guilty Mosque

*Kashf*

*the uncovery; the removal of the veil;
revealing the reality beneath*

## Asrar

*My name means 'secrets' and these are what I keep. When I walk in the desert, these are what I hear. When I pray to God, this is what I'm told. I have a name for every one of my fireflies and they sleep outside my door. They took me to the mosque this morning where I watched Ruhiya cry and where I heard her sing. It made me tall and old. There are secrets in the mosque now that no one can explain, and the door has been locked. Yehya has been waiting in God's house over the valley and calling out her name, night after night calling straight into my dreams, where I kept his secret. The monks are hiding him, and have given him a robe. It's brown and yellow. At night they sit together at a long table and dine on rice soup and fresh dates.*

*Before midday I washed mint and cleaned the rice for lunch. I prepared a salad with thyme, chopped onion and lemon pieces, and hung the yoghurt to strain over the sink. In the kitchen Ruhiya's voice carried through the water even as it went down the drain and when I said this, no one believed me. They said, 'Asrar has the imagination of a witch.'*

*She made me promise not to tell what I saw.*

'Cross your heart and swear on the Qur'an.' *I didn't. There was no secret.*

*When I see a communion of lizards, I go; I know to follow the animals when there is more than one, more than two; when it's dark, their sparkling eyes lay jewels and stretch out a road before me.*

*After our conversation Ruhiya turned around and walked away. I watched her as she became smaller and I ran home with joy. Later, I would tiptoe over the crumble of spirits hiding in the sand, run past the faces frozen in the desert rock and wait for the lizards to crawl out from underneath the stones. At midday, when the sun was high and there were no shadows on the mountains I ran and hid from Ruhiya just as soon as I found her. She was by a small stream where she washed her hands, face and feet. She splashed and sprinkled the water and drank from it. Then she laid her hijab on the floor and, with her loose, damp hair falling about her shoulders, prostrated herself for prayer. She held her upturned palms together and I imagined her lips silently giving alms. At the end she whispered: 'You who guides us on our path, show us the road to Paradise,' and repeated it a hundred times. When she was finished, her hair was dry. She threw her* veil, which had been stained by the sand and appeared pink, loosely about her hair and disappeared at once, into the rocks like a lizard. But nothing can protect you from death.

A large iguana, three foot long, spoke to me. I had walked without seeing him for miles, along a tarmac road, past the Bedouin tents, until I reached the canyon and the monastery embraced between its cliff walls. There I saw Yehya and his soul was shattered. He stood on the terraces with the monks who consoled him and wiped his tears and offered him the sweet drink from their vines to lighten his spirits. As the sky grew darker they lit torches and led him inside through an arcade and into a cool labyrinth of corridors. I felt his feet pressing against the thick carpets inside like the lips of God on my heart.

My mother told me later with a kiss, 'There are no iguanas here, Asrar.' She's right, there aren't; but one had come to me.

When I was six years old I stopped speaking for two years, refused to go to school, and started to hear better. I stopped looking, and closed my eyes, and saw everything. I saw what the Honeyman did to Hurra, how he had unveiled her, and what she *did to herself, and I kept their secret. The amulets she made and the one she carried with her couldn't protect her, because no charm can keep you from dying inside, from dying at all, from the witchcraft, once it's in your blood.*

*Some things don't exist. But badness does.*

*Farhan grew fat after her death, swelled up like he had been stung by all of his ferocious bees, and cried in his sleep when only I could hear him. His bees produced so much honey Yehya's father started to sell it all over the west bank of the Jordan River in Jerusalem, Qalkilya, Tulkarem, Nablus and Jenin. So much honey, he soon had to put it in large jars and send it. Inside, to the coastal towns I can only ever dream about, to Jaffa, Acre, Haifa...*

*So much sweetness in the land.*

*But nothing can keep you from dying inside. No honeycomb can keep you from your own witchcraft.*

*Hurra's luminous skin grew dim but she was transparent. One night al-Ashkar sat up by candlelight and wrote a* hijab *for her in red ink. Then he shut the booklet, and marked the brown leather cover with a pounding heart. He loosened his long white hair and sat up in his chair for hours as the cool light of the moon travelled across his face.*

*The old people who came from the coast long for the length in their stride. In those days what was Palestine but a stop on the road to Lebanon? I try to imagine, but my eyes won't let me see... They say that as you approached Jaffa in the spring, there was a balm to greet you from the orange and lemon groves as powerful as bottled essence. They say that you could stand in the lush gardens of Haifa in the north and look out to the mountains of Lebanon, and that the walls of the city of Acre reached right down to the sea. And in the summer, the sea was gracious enough to let you sleep by her side, and made you feel like a sultan with his favourite wife. The salty spray, the invisible, weightless blanket, made you dream of love affairs of the sweetest kind.*

*The old people say they would have fled to Gaza thirty years ago had they known they were not going back to be fishermen again. At least in the refugee camps of Gaza you could sit in open sewage and look over barbed wire to the water beyond and imagine the coastline to Alexandria.*

*I would listen to their stories and memorize every word, reciting them to myself at night. They even say that on some summer nights, the tide would rise in the motionless, still Mediterranean and bring new gifts, laying them in the cast nets at the beach's feet, and bloating the fishermen with pride. That was their secret.*

*How could I possibly protect her from the curse that killed her mother, from the tears they say the angels are shedding, from the jinn's laugh, from the fire that will surely come? When Hurra's pain became too great, she flapped her wings once and flew away, into the darkness like a bat.*

*A Bedouin man came to the village the same day and said:* 'The Arabs are shrouding their women from the sun. My people come from the Steppes of Tadmoor. We are blood-bound and sure-footed and can help you with your sorrow.' *He wore a wide black garment made of camel hair over a long white shirt. He unfurled his turban after he spoke to reveal a dark, oval face and a shiny black moustache. He pulled a carved knife from his leather belt, sat down and laid it beside him. Hurra's husband poured him a cup of coffee and a glass of water and said to the man:* 'My wife is dead, and you are speaking with a poetic voice. Don't you know that nothing will avenge her death. I don't know why she died or who made her weep but as God is my witness I will purify her soul with my prayers, I will perform the *adhan*

78

for Hurra even if I am on my knees; I will sing to her with my last breath and she will rest in peace.' 'I beg you, Sheikh Radwan,' *the Bedouin man looked at him with pity.* 'We can investigate what happened, we can find a way to reconcile the community. You cannot carry your wife's blood on your own, God have mercy on her soul. Whoever is responsible shall compensate you and wrap your house with white silk. Your name is precious to us, Sheikh Radwan, and you have a daughter to think about, may God guard her and keep her by your side. The earth and the stone on which this village is built cannot absorb an injury to your honour. It will remain a stain.'

*But Radwan knew that an investigation would break his spirit, that the truth would break his heart, because he had not protected Hurra.* 'Sir, I don't mean to offend you, but the only reconciliation to be made is with God, and I will make it my duty, for as long as I breathe, to achieve it.' *The Bedouin man did not touch the drink that Radwan had offered him.* 'May God grant you a long life, Sheikh Radwan.'

*Her husband was inconsolable. Radwan cried so much that after forty days the dry village well filled up, and I hear the adults complain even today that*

79

*they are drinking the water of the Dead Sea, the village water is so dense with salt. Nobody ever mentioned her death again in public; nobody looked at Yehya's father with accusing eyes, but the whispers continued, and he grew fatter...*

*The crescent moon had risen and the sun was beginning its descent so I left my mother and aunts to perform the afternoon prayers, which they had to guess by looking at the shadows against the hills. They spoke loudly about this and argued at great length. When they agreed that it was, most probably, time for Salat al-Asr, they headed for the spring behind our house for the ablutions, all the while pretending that they couldn't be sure of the exact time, lamenting that God would surely sympathize with this unexpected state of affairs, that punctuality was an essential component of religious observance, but that this couldn't be helped and God relieve the soul of the mad girl who had spoilt a holy place. They weren't saying Ruhiya's name. I tailed the afternoon shadows along the walls towards the centre of the village and the mosque, so quiet now and closed. I stopped to look at the green iron door that I had never before seen shut.*

'The girl's been pulled to heaven by her tongue.'

'You mean to hell...'

*There were men's voices coming from inside, speaking in heated whispers.*

'And her father's fever has lifted. Has the girl performed a miracle?'

'A miracle?! You blaspheme! It is taboo for a woman to raise her voice! Now she has raised it for all to hear, without shame, and worse she has done so in God's name. Oh, I never thought I would live to see a day as unlucky as this. If we don't do the right thing, who knows what will come next?'

'By God the compassionate, Hurra herself will be turning in her grave...'

'I agree. This is a sign, a sign from God that our community has been polluted and must be cleansed. The soldiers were laughing at us today, pretending they had merely come to arrest some men! May they all be struck down by high blood pressure and diabetes! I wouldn't be surprised if this was their work, that there has been some collaboration with the enemy. A woman immodest enough to display her ecstasy to the entire world! She is obviously the perfect accessory for the Zionists...'

'...Indeed, why should she stop at the Zionists?'

*The room fell silent. Words were settling. Grown-ups are misguided. They guard against the Devil in all the wrong places. They were grunting and sighing. There was a feeling of suffocation. What if they decided that Ruhiya was influenced by darker forces? Someone cleared his throat to speak.*

'Dearest friends, we must talk to the *muezzin* himself. He is a man of great integrity who has endured much grief. I am anxious that we do not cause him distress for he is frail and has been exemplary in his behaviour his entire life. Let us not forget that it is his gentle voice that has beckoned us and our children and our grandchildren to prayer, and we must approach him with sanctity in our hearts. For he is a part of us and we are a part of him.'

*It was my grandfather, the one they call al-Ashkar because of the paleness of his skin and colourless hair. Even the holy man everyone agreed was incapable of sin, because he did not have the pigment, could not clear the air. Hurra's men were bloodthirsty.*

'Exemplary! How can you grant him this honour? What kind of a man does not avenge his wife's death and would rather sweep the whole affair under the carpet? What kind of a man does not want to shred the heart of the beast who violated his own wife? I am telling you, Sheikh Radwan – may God cure him of the disease that ails his heart, may He absolve him – will be destroyed by his own conscience yet. But we can help him now, and we must do something to restore his repute, for this has gone too far, and this is the final proof.'

'I agree. We must restore his repute as well as our own self-respect. We are Arabs and we are brothers. I myself will not stand helplessly whilst the Bedouins and Jews laugh at us. We must prove that we too are honour-bound. I suggest that tonight we go to the *muezzin's* house and discuss a way to settle this. He is no longer the only one implicated in this crime. This is a matter for all of us now.'

*I stood to one side of the mosque as the men came out, shaking hands and embracing. My grandfather let the others go on ahead of him and when they were far enough he called out to me.*

'Asrar! I know you're hiding! Come let us go and pay our respects to Umm Eid. She has lost her boy.'

*I walked up to my grandfather with my head lowered in shame for eavesdropping and having been discovered. I took the bony hand that he had* raised for me to kiss and pressed it to my lips.

'You're a good girl, Asrar. Even if you have big ears, you have an even bigger heart.'

Now that the soldiers were gone, the village streets were filling once again with people as they headed for the martyr's house to give their thanks and praises. I could hear the women ululating, rejoicing in the certain knowledge that the eternal light would forever shine on the beloved. But as I walked next to my grandfather my eyes filled involuntarily with tears, because Eid is dead, and Yehya has disappeared.

Even though I am scared, I want to find Ruhiya and her brother, the siblings of Farhan's split seed. My grandfather left me to lead the mourners in prayers for the martyr and I slipped again out of the house. But a fear had overcome me and was drowning out the earth's whispers. I walked farther away, thinking that the animals were probably confused by the events of the day. When I could no longer see the trees of al-Ahmar I stopped and looked around one last time for them but they did not come. My belly suddenly felt full and painful. I felt a trickle of something thick and sticky slide down my inner thigh, and I looked down to find little red pearls of fresh blood.

I touch it, taste it.

The journalist was right, the desert is big.

# The Honeyman's Remembrance

*Kheshya*

*fear of God, which brings man closer to
holiness*

## Farhan, Abu Yehya

*My destiny dismembered me.*

*And my boy? I hear my boy shaved his head, threw out his clothes and roamed with caravans barefoot. I hear he was seen laughing with girls with bare faces, that he learnt the songs of the nomadic tribes and the Aramaic of the Syrians. I hear that the soles of his feet are shredded, that he is bleeding all over the plains of the Middle East, and crossing borders like a gypsy as though they didn't exist. But he was always a master at that.*

*I hear he may be herding goats and that no charge is too heavy for Yehya, the wild, imperceptible one, transformed again. Some burdens cannot be shed and make their bearers stronger. My boy is alive but will he come back from the dead?*

Last night, another impossible, real dream of love. The Free Woman, Hurra, my love who had left me came back. Stood at the edge of my bed. Faced me squarely. I do love you. An embrace. That's all there is to it. But you're so frightening. That's how I've always been. Blue eyes. Dark skin. Greying hair. It's Hurra come to me again.

Hurra was born in the fertile hills around

Bethlehem and wasn't used to the lowest plains of the earth around the Dead Sea. The first day she arrived at al-Ahmar, she trailed behind the *muezzin* like a scent. Her heavy black veil, embroidered in silver thread, framed a face conceived in alabaster and her eyelashes were cast so low she looked as though she were sleepwalking. And nothing in the witch hinted at the indigo eyes.

Her bridegroom reached back for her with his hand and she was suddenly looking up, back at me and she kind of swooned as the heat overcame her and subdued her pulse into a slow faint. I don't remember her reaching the ground, just the falling. It had something of the orange night to it, and the voluptuousness of the summer trees. I had collided with her.

Radwan gathered his woman into his thick arms and carried her to the village well, where he sat her down, scooped cool water out of a bucket and drizzled it on to her raised face. They laughed together then.

Even though it was early in the season and their flow had not stopped, that day I harvested the treasures from my bees. In the garden I lit a ball of paper and approached the hives quietly so as not to alert the colonies. As the smoke drifted inside I suddenly realized I had forgotten my gloves and veil. I had yet to be stung by one of my bees.

That year the orange trees had blossomed well before they were due and I had expected a darker hue to my honey. But nothing prepared me for the shade of maroon that looked like it had coagulated on the comb.

I removed the combs and carried them inside. With my silver knife I uncapped the hexagonal cells, extracted the larvae and the condensed nectar and walked to the *muezzin*'s house the same evening, with an earthenware jug of my bees' darkest baby food for the newlyweds. When I stood in the doorway Radwan enveloped me in his great expansive frame and pulled me into the candlelit house out of the twilight. 'Hurra, come greet Farhan, Abu Yehya.' He had a bellowing, smooth voice, welcome as warm water on a cool morning. 'He brings us an offering from his bees.' The bride walked in then so sensationally slow and proud, and stuck her long hand out for mine to shake. The dark brown patterns of henna upon it seemed to be dancing in the shadows of the flames. This time her face was surrounded by a chaos of black curls which rose and fell with every breath. Thick lines of freshly applied kohl rimmed her eyes.

'Would that be honey, Abu Yehya, or venom?' She looked straight at me when she said that, and then turned to her husband with a wide smile. I was sure she could hear my heart rebelling against the confinement of its cage and that she was baiting, taunting me. But somehow my back remained erect even though my spine was crumbling and I steadied my gaze on the *muezzin*'s beautiful face. 'Madam, it is the purest honey snatched from my bees for your prosperity...' There was an awkward silence as the atmosphere in the room changed. I had overreacted, taken her words too seriously and my reply had been too forceful. Then the *muezzin*, without any malice or suspicion, but simply because an opportunity to praise God had arisen, started to recite from Surat al-Nahl: *'Then to eat of all the produce of the earth and follow the way of thy Lord made smooth: there issues from within their bodies a drink of varying colours, wherein is healing for men: verily in this is a Sign for those who give thought.'* (Qur'an 16:69.) I looked at him with the gratitude of a hungry thief who, having been caught, is shown mercy by an afluent landowner and allowed to run off with the fruit stolen from his orchard. Was he blind, or was Radwan's own heart as tender as that of the palm tree? It wouldn't be the last time that his kindness diverted attention from my guilt.

*Would that be honey, Abu Yehya, or venom?* The words had poured from her mouth like a gift, like a curse as I stood barefoot and helpless on the cool tiles in Radwan's house. I had brought her honey red like the carnelian stone, red like the earth I was born to and live off, red like a dull fire in the sky. It was there that my heart slipped from me, as insignificantly as a hair being carried out to sea. I was branded by a virgin seer with tinted hands and feet on the day of her marriage. I held the darkest intention for Hurra and rested in its shade. I should have been restrained there and then as I stood on the threshold of her home with honey on my hands and blood in my eyes. There was a war going on inside, transforming me into a mangle of fear and lust. When she spoke my whole being hung on her voice, at once so sweet and severe she could have been instructing angels and collaborating with the underworld in the same breath. But even as she stood before me I knew I would break through the metallic screen. I thought of the seven gates of

Jerusalem's wall, of the temples of worship inside, and of the seven orifices on Hurra's body. I suddenly remembered Him and shuddered. Other apertures, unspoken of, came to mind. The thought of the slit on each of her nipples inflamed me. Hurra laughed out loud then for I must have looked horrified, and her laughter lashed out like hot oil.

It was summer, and I watched her daily after that from behind my beekeeper's screen veil. Hurra may have appeared delicate but she was tenacious, and she flourished in the desert like a luxuriant aloe fulfilling the potential of the oasis. Over time I drew closer, inching towards her through invisible passages, interlocking each step with hers. I was quiet and undetectable until suddenly I was there, holding her to me. I buried my face in the mass of hair that smelt like a winter wood-fire, inhaled the faint aroma of roasted chestnuts that emanated from her skin. Hurra had nowhere to go, I had brought her home. Her arms grew tired of pushing me. My palms left imprints on her back and my fingers fastened around her hair. The sharp angles of her elbows fit snugly beneath my jaw and when I finally pinned her down, her knees jammed against my waist. Hurra. The statue of spirit, the sadness of Magdalene. I can't believe she died, bled, birthed. Into my reserves of energy I devoured her like oxygen. She said, 'Time will tell, Abu Yehya, what you have done.'

And time told. She was a strange victim.

I sought her everywhere, and although she evaded me, I found her every time. Alone, stretching the morning's washing on the clothesline, carrying warm milk in her brass teapot or walking to draw water from the well. I felt I was being steered by a supernatural information, in the same way that bees, guided by some miraculous knowledge, seek out inaccessible places in which to build their cells. And when I found her I faced her like a dog at the portals of paradise craving delivery into the garden of pious souls. I marvelled at my own abasement but continued to pursue her with the same compulsion. I grew fiercer, causing cries of pain and shame I came to endure, more aggressive as a desire to regress into the Sefer got a grip on me. I wanted her to carry us there, to traverse time and meet me again at the beginning, to span back to the flipside of the sun and the original mirror image of the universe.

And who's to say I wasn't right, that I wasn't fulfilling a higher will, unpredictable and immovable? God's will be done, I thought it was the way of the warrior to go, to lose myself, and then I froze.

If it were possible to steal energy then I stole, for I was hungry and cold, and drank more blood than I could hold. My breath grew in her and the last unshed tear remained behind, and Hurra's Christ finally abandoned her. I had gutted and filled her. Sometimes I like to imagine I understood her. That she craved me as I craved her, that I found her, woke her, saved her. That she kissed me, when I kissed her. She throbbed in me and something in me convinced me that something in her longed for me.

And then the little girl arrived, a testament to the phenomena of grace, with the same high brow as her mother, though her eyes were a golden-brown like mine, the Honeyman with the bloodshot eyes. And this is what they said: *'Her memory rises in his eyes like steam. The Honeyman can't live any more, he can only dream.'* Now the sand is damp and the sun is close to setting and a shiver runs down my spine like a river and revives a pain that's worth forgetting.

I was in a groove, trapped in the deepest depression on the surface of the earth, like the Dead Sea itself without release or escape or a lifeline. I continued to search for her as though she were still alive. I search for her every hour unto this day – in the sky, in the streams, in the trees. In the ice cold morning and in the afternoon breeze.

The last time I saw her, Hurra said to me, 'Don't talk to me, I'm unstoppable. You were an encounter in the night. Now I want my freedom.' The exalted virgin of my tumultuous nightmares was melting before me, she was that close to the fire. Later we looked together for a rope and when we found one her voice was steady but hollow as she whispered, 'It's rough,' and stood still, so close to me. I didn't matter any more, her eyes were drifting as fast as her pain and I was spellbound to my destiny. It was not a time for tying up loose ends, it was a point on a circle. In my endeavours to transgress time and defy space I was caught between two skies, between the twilight and the sun.

Hurra stood herself in front of me and held the noose behind her back. She placed it carefully around her neck, shook her head and spat at me. 'You poisoned me.' Technically I killed her. If it were a matter of grabbing her, with my dirty hands I would have brought her back. But my heart was in a hair, and it was lost at sea. I don't recall who it was who came upon the body but it was still warm and Hurra was buried a few hours later. For the first time in the history of the village a female was reluctantly allowed to attend a burial. Ruhiya stared any objections down with her long, shiny stare, as the men of the village gathered for the interment, all the while holding on to Radwan's hand and he holding back the tears.

At first I walked in fear, then I lived in dread. The gloating stares of the villagers bit my wounds like salted water. Even though I carried on breathing, I lived on borrowed courage and fed from an indiscernible pool of compassion. My days were dark, the heart was overcast. The name of God the Merciful was far from my lips. I was confined to a room with the ceiling painted black as a woman's womb.

But today I offer my own palms to the sun and to the rain. I rejoice, I grieve. For when the earth was still and quiet, voices fed on it started rising. And it may sound like water gushing from a spring, until pieces of broken rock go flying. And it was through this tremor of the earth that my daughter's voice came, and it could not be contoured and it cannot be defined. I heard her song spiral and then unwind as she resolutely called the dormant ones, recalled the spirits trapped in a grave. She brandished her arms, dancing like an enchantress around the sanctuary where her childhood was embalmed. Ruhiya, who grew up with her back turned to a secret fetish that can never be repeated, floated under the hour until the circle was complete and re-emerged transformed into the litmus flower of her mother's spirit.

Don't we have children, after all is said and done, to divert attention from our own mortality?

I talk the talk of a living man. I seek redemption. I tread to gravitational places, shifting myself from breath to breath like a burglar in a palace. If they were here they would hear me, I'm screaming; they would feel me, I'm cold. I'm weighed down and slowed down by a ball and chain of iron and I pull around the pain with me, everywhere I go.

# Epilogue

The fuzz on my skull was grey and covered in frozen sweat beads. It felt like my cranium had been skinned.

I was heading for the Land of the Dead and moved north, east, to more intense colds than I had ever imagined. I sold silk and carried silver across mountain ranges and rice fields. To peoples with a dark-pink complexion and old teachings. There they said a story had been told of a sister and a brother, and of a sacred date palm that had sprung up in the place where she had fallen. Mistaking me for one of their own, they warned me against coming face to face with him, a Canaanite fierce as the white man, graceful as the black.

They warned me of crossing too many horizons and of getting lost on the other side: but then the constellations rearranged themselves and once again I fled, I flew. I picked seashells off the bottom of a jungle floor and came upon a city carved in light, dreamt up by a dwarf sorcerer. There I remained and was tutored in the Art of the Shadows by old women with scarred faces, until one misty dawn, I engraved my sister's name in air.

I was drenched in magic.

I learnt the language of the tongue, of the throat,

of the lips and of the drum. Women tiptoed across my path and left a discernible sheath in their wake. As prayer beads dissolved in my hands and red nuts tinted my teeth, I learnt to love without longing and courted my destiny with resolve.

Was it the climate or the seasons that changed? I got used to the cold.

My body was strong, I was ready for my tribe. Like a heavenly tree I was reaching for the soil. The Pine and the Sandalwood, the Cypress and the Palm, the Cedar all inside me.

I didn't turn back, I returned home with a sunken chest and swollen heart, with tendons like iron wire. Where's the fool, where's the wise man, on this planet paved with conversations with the father? I walked in earnest, mindfully, at ease. Dirt glittered in the sunshine. Something led me there. A blessed memory flickered like a revived fire. A shadow rebelling against the light. In a turbulence she came. With her back turned to me she said, *'Stay, for once,'* and she was gone and left me face to face with him. I laid down the remnants of the load that had clung to me. This is where I started. This is where I stop.

I held on. She came again. We stood on the side of the hill overlooking al-Ahmar the way we had when we were children, with my blood running through her and her voice running through me. She said, *'Yehya, they have waited for you, and I have guarded them.'* But I didn't believe her until I saw for myself the oasis, swarming with particles of gold. Am I happy. I replied that my heart was intact. What about my soul, she asked? It was soaring, and it was normally impenetrable. *'And did you meet idols, on your journey?'* I replied, *'I met idols, I built icons for my fear.'*

Ruhiya, I will always love you, my lioness!

I leant against the date palm and closed my dry eyes. I sense God everywhere. I can't tell him from another.

Perhaps I will go back to the monks, and ask for a prayer for my father.